PETER RABBIT'S
NATURAL FOODS COOKBOOK

The "PETER RABBIT" BOOKS
by BEATRIX POTTER

PETER RABBIT · SQUIRREL NUTKIN
TAILOR OF GLOUCESTER · BENJAMIN BUNNY
TWO BAD MICE · MRS. TIGGY – WINKLE
MR. JEREMY FISHER · TOM KITTEN
JEMIMA PUDDLE-DUCK · THE FLOPSY BUNNIES
MRS. TITTLEMOUSE · TIMMY TIPTOES
JOHNNY TOWN-MOUSE · MR. TOD
PIGLING BLAND · SAMUEL WHISKERS
THE PIE & THE PATTY-PAN · GINGER & PICKLES
LITTLE PIG ROBINSON

A FIERCE BAD RABBIT	MISS MOPPET
APPLEY DAPPLY'S	CECILY PARSLEY'S
NURSERY RHYMES	NURSERY RHYMES
PETER RABBIT'S	TOM KITTEN'S
PAINTING BOOK	PAINTING BOOK

ILLUSTRATED BY BEATRIX POTTER

PETER RABBIT'S
NATURAL FOODS COOKBOOK

BY ARNOLD DOBRIN

FREDERICK WARNE

NEW YORK • LONDON

For Nellie, Hilda and Bettina—*who showed the way*

The author wishes to express his grateful appreciation to Carolyn Meyer for her help in the preparation of this book.

Cover Design after an illustration by Beatrix Potter

Text Copyright © 1977 Arnold Dobrin
Design and Illustration Copyright © 1977, 1976, 1974, 1971, 1958, 1957, 1955, 1946, 1941, 1940, 1939, 1938, 1937, 1936, 1935, 1934, 1933, 1932, 1931, 1929, 1905 Frederick Warne & Co., New York and London

Frederick Warne & Co., Inc.
New York, New York

Manufactured in the United States of America
Library of Congress Catalog Card Number: 76-45309
ISBN: 0-7232-6142-3

Design by Peter Landa
Composition by Frost Bros., Inc.

10   11   12   13   14   89   88   87   86   85

PREFACE

When I was growing up, the animals inhabiting the magical world created by Beatrix Potter made a deep and abiding impression on my mind. Even now, as I recall those years, I can almost smell the delicious scents of the English fields and orchards; I can almost taste the wonderful flavor of their fresh fruits and vegetables.

It was the world of Beatrix Potter that inspired this cookbook. I hope you will find that the foods you make have the same simple goodness that I—and so many others—associate with Peter Rabbit and the other Potter characters. I hope, too, that you will enjoy them and want to explore other dishes prepared primarily from grain, fruit, and vegetables.

If you eat nourishing foods, and do not overeat, I doubt that you will ever have to be put to bed, as was poor Peter, with a cup of hot chamomile tea.

—ARNOLD DOBRIN

5

CONTENTS

A WORD ABOUT EQUIPMENT

Knives, electric blenders and mixers can be dangerous. Never use a sharp knife or a blender unless you have assistance from an adult. When learning to cook, it's important to have adult supervision when using the stove or the oven, too.

Always pick up a knife firmly by the handle, and concentrate on what you are doing. Learn which knives are best to use for a particular kind of cutting. For example, bread knives should be used for sandwiches. Paring knives are best for cutting fruit and vegetables. And remember that all cutting or chopping should be done on a wooden board. For further instructions about using knives, please consult the "How To Chop" section on page 107.

BREAKFAST
AND BREADS

SAMUEL WHISKERS'
ROLY-POLY PANCAKES

EQUIPMENT

medium-sized mixing bowl
fork
measuring cups and spoons
rotary beater

griddle
ladle
paper towel
spatula

INGREDIENTS

¾ cup unbleached white flour
¼ cup whole-wheat flour
¼ cup corn meal
  (*or: 1 cup unbleached white
      flour*
    ¼ cup corn meal)
2 teaspoons baking powder
2 teaspoons sugar

½ teaspoon salt
¼ teaspoon nutmeg
1 egg
1 cup milk
2 tablespoons vegetable oil
dab of butter, shortening,
  or margarine

Put the white flour, whole-wheat flour, corn meal, baking powder, sugar, salt, and nutmeg into a mixing bowl and stir them lightly with a fork until they are thoroughly mixed.

Add the egg, milk, and vegetable oil to the mixture. Beat with a rotary beater until the batter is smooth and creamy.

Meanwhile, heat the griddle. To find out when it is hot enough, sprinkle it with a few drops of water. If the drops dance and skitter around, the griddle is ready. Put a dab of shortening on a crumpled-up paper towel and grease the griddle lightly. Be careful, because the griddle is hot.

Pour the batter on the griddle with a ladle, leaving space between each pancake so they don't run together. When the pancakes are bubbly in the center and dry around the edges, turn them over with a spatula and cook them for one more minute.

Makes about 12 four-inch pancakes.

TIMMY WILLIE'S SUNNY
SUNDAY SCRAMBLED EGGS

EQUIPMENT

small pan of boiling water
slotted spoon
sharp knife

small mixing bowl
fork
skillet

INGREDIENTS

4 eggs
2 tablespoons butter or
    margarine
salt and pepper and any of the
    following extras:
    1 small tomato
    2 tablespoons sliced
       mushrooms

1-2 tablespoons chopped
    scallions (green onions)
1 tablespoon grated
    Parmesan cheese
2 tablespoons cheddar or
    Swiss cheese, cut up in
    small cubes
1 tablespoon chopped fresh
    parsley or chives

First, prepare the extras, choosing one from the list, or any combination that you like. To prepare the tomato, dip it for a few moments in a pan of boiling water, remove with a slotted spoon, and pull off the skin. Then cut it in four chunks and drain off the juice and seeds (save for soup). Chop the tomato pulp and cook quickly in 1 teaspoon of hot butter or margarine in a separate pan. Set the tomato aside.

To cook the mushrooms, wash them in cold water and wipe dry with a paper towel. Slice or chop them and cook them in a

skillet for three minutes in a teaspoon of hot butter or margarine. Set them aside.

To cook the scallions, wash, chop, and cook for two minutes in a little butter.

Break the eggs into a mixing bowl and beat them with a fork lightly if you like gold and white eggs, thoroughly if you like them really scrambled.

Heat the butter or margarine in a skillet over low heat. When it is melted and bubbling, pour in the egg mixture. Cook the eggs slowly, stirring them gently while they cook. Sprinkle with salt and pepper.

When they are almost set, add the extras, folding them in gently. When the eggs are cooked through but are still moist and shiny, serve them immediately.

Serves 2 to 3.

SQUIRREL NUTKIN'S BANANA-NUT LOAF

EQUIPMENT

2 medium-sized mixing bowls
fork
measuring cups and spoons
mixing spoon
9 x 5 x 3-inch loaf pan

plastic scraper
pot holders
wire rack
spatula

INGREDIENTS

2 ripe bananas
3/4 cup sugar
2 tablespoons soft vegetable
    shortening
1 egg
3/4 cup milk or orange juice
3 cups unbleached flour

(or: 1 cup unbleached flour
1 cup whole-wheat flour
3/4 cup oatmeal
1/4 cup wheat germ)
4 teaspoons baking powder
1 teaspoon salt
3/4 cup chopped nuts, raisins,
    or chopped dates or figs if
    you like them.

In one mixing bowl, mash the ripe bananas with a fork. Add the sugar, shortening, and egg and mix well with a mixing spoon. Gradually stir in the milk or orange juice.

In another mixing bowl put the flour (or the two kinds of flour, oatmeal, and wheat germ), baking powder, and salt. Stir them lightly with a fork until they are thoroughly mixed.

Add the dry ingredients to the banana mixture and stir until they are completely blended. Add the nuts, raisins, dates, or figs if you like them.

Grease the loaf pan thoroughly with extra shortening. Pour the batter into the pan, spreading it higher in the corners with the plastic scraper.

18

Turn the oven on to 350 degrees. Let the pan stand for twenty minutes while the oven heats. Bake the loaf for an hour and 10 minutes.

Using the pot holders, take the pan out of the oven and set it on a wire rack to cool. When it is cool enough to handle, carefully loosen the edges of the loaf with a spatula and take the loaf out of the pan. Let it cool completely on the wire rack. Wrap it in plastic or aluminum foil. To keep it from crumbling, slice it with a thin sharp knife only after it has cooled completely—over night, if you can wait that long.

Makes 1 loaf.

PIGLING AND PIGWIG'S
HOT RICE BREAKFAST TREAT

medium-sized saucepan with
   lid

measuring cups and spoons

INGREDIENTS

2 cups leftover cooked rice
   (or ⅔ cup uncooked rice
   and 1⅓ cups water)
1 small tart apple
2 cups milk
¼ cup brown sugar

½ cup raisins or chopped
   dried fruit, such as apricots
   or dates
½ teaspoon cinnamon
dash of salt

If you are using uncooked rice, put the rice and water in a saucepan, turn the burner on to medium-high, and bring the rice and water to a boil. Turn the heat to low, put the lid on the saucepan, and let the rice simmer for 15 minutes.

Meanwhile, wash the apple, but you don't need to peel it. Cut it into four quarters, cut away the core, and cut the apple into small pieces. Add the apple to the cooked rice.

Add the milk, brown sugar, raisins or other fruit, cinnamon, and salt. Cook slowly, stirring often, for ten minutes.

Serves 4.

NOTE: You can add these same ingredients to other cooked cereals, such as oatmeal, Cream of Wheat, and Wheatina.

JOHNNY TOWN-MOUSE'S GRANOLA

medium-sized mixing bowl
measuring cups and spoons
mixing spoon
sharp knife

cookie sheet or large baking
pan
pot holders
hot mat or wire rack

2 cups oatmeal
½ cup wheat germ
¼ teaspoon salt
2 tablespoons vegetable oil
¼ cup honey
any or all of the following
    extra ingredients making
    a total of one cup:

chopped nuts (almonds are
    good)
unsweetened grated coconut
sesame seeds
sunflower seeds, unsalted
chopped dried apples
chopped dried apricots
raisins

Turn on the oven and let it heat to 250 degrees.

Put the oatmeal, wheat germ, and salt in a mixing bowl and stir. Add vegetable oil and honey. Spread the mixture on a cookie

22

sheet or large baking pan. Bake for 30 minutes.

Take the cookie sheet out of the oven and set it on a hot mat or wire rack. Add whatever extra ingredients you are using, except for raisins, stirring carefully. Bake for 15 minutes more (longer if you like the coconut toasty).

Take the cookie sheet out of the oven and set it on the wire rack again. Stir in the raisins if you are using them. Let the mixture cool, stirring it once while it cools. Store in a container with a tight cover, or in a plastic bag.

Makes about 4 cups.

TOMMY BROCK AND MR. TOD'S
WHEAT GERM MUFFINS

EQUIPMENT

muffin pans for 12 muffins
2 medium-sized mixing bowls
fork
measuring cups and spoons
mixing spoon

plastic scraper
pot holders
wire rack
table knife

INGREDIENTS

vegetable shortening, butter,
   or margarine
1 egg
¼ cup sugar
1 cup milk

¼ cup vegetable oil
1 cup unbleached white flour
1 cup wheat germ
2½ teaspoons baking powder
½ teaspoon salt

Turn on the oven and let it heat to 425 degrees. Grease each muffin cup thoroughly with the vegetable shortening, butter, or margarine, or put a paper muffin liner in each cup.

Put the egg in one mixing bowl and beat it with a fork. Beat in the sugar, milk, and vegetable oil.

In another mixing bowl put the flour, wheat germ, salt, and baking powder. Stir them lightly with a fork until they are thoroughly mixed.

Add the dry ingredients to the egg and milk mixture and stir

until they are just blended. The batter should be lumpy. Don't mix it too much or the muffins won't be light and fluffy.

Fill each muffin cup ⅔ full. Bake for 15 minutes, or until the tops are golden brown. Using pot holders, take the muffin pans out of the oven. Use a table knife to loosen each muffin around the sides. Lift them out of the cups to cool on the wire rack.

Makes 12 muffins.

SANDWICHES

ALDER-RAT SQUEAKER'S HOMEMADE PEANUT BUTTER

EQUIPMENT

baking sheet   blender
measuring cup and spoons   plastic scraper

INGREDIENTS

2 cups shelled peanuts (dry-   about 1 tablespoon vegetable
   roasted, roasted in the shell,   oil
   or raw)   about 1 teaspoon salt

Dry-roasted peanuts are easiest to use, because they are already prepared. Peanuts roasted in the shell only need to have their shells and skins removed. To roast raw peanuts, remove the shells and skins and place them on a baking sheet that has been coated with vegetable oil.

    Preheat the oven to 350 degrees and bake the peanuts for about 15 minutes, stirring them every 5 minutes, until they are golden brown. Some people prefer to make peanut butter with raw nuts.

Whichever kind you use, put the peanuts—1 cup at a time—in the container of the blender, put on the lid, and run the blender at medium speed for about ten seconds until the nuts are roughly chopped.

Turn off the blender, remove the lid, and use the scraper to push the nuts from around the sides of the container down into the blades. Put the lid back on, and run the blender at a higher speed for about 5 seconds. If the blender motor seems to be working too hard and the nuts are not forming a paste, turn off the blender and add 1 tablespoon of vegetable oil. Again, push the nuts down into the blades.

Put the lid back on and run the blender at high speed for 5 seconds more, or until a grainy peanut butter is formed. Taste the peanut butter and add salt if it needs it.

Makes 1 cup of peanut butter.

LITTLE PIG ROBINSON'S PEANUT BUTTER SANDWICHES

EQUIPMENT

measuring cups and spoons
small mixing bowl
fork
sharp knife
table knife for spreading

INGREDIENTS

[1] ⅓ cup peanut butter
1 tablespoon sesame seeds
1 tablespoon chopped celery

[2] ⅓ cup peanut butter
1 tablespoon lemon juice
1 tablespoon raisins

[3] ⅓ cup peanut butter
1 tablespoon chopped cashews, or other nuts
1 tablespoon shredded coconut

Make these three types of sandwiches with thin slices of Banana-Nut Loaf (page 17) or with any whole-grain bread. Each recipe makes enough filling for 2 or 3 sandwiches.

Put all the ingredients of the filling you choose in a small bowl and mix well. Spread on slices of bread. Add a lettuce leaf to each sandwich if you wish, and top with a second slice of bread.

Here are two more peanut-butter combination sandwiches:

[4] peanut butter   tomato slices
    mayonnaise   cucumber slices

Toast bread. Spread peanut butter on one slice and mayonnaise on the other. Put together with slices of tomato and cucumber.

[5] peanut butter   banana slices
    lettuce

Spread peanut butter thinly on each slice of bread. Put together with lettuce and banana slices.

MR. PRICKLEPIN'S CREAM OR COTTAGE CHEESE SANDWICHES

EQUIPMENT

measuring cups and spoons
small mixing bowl
fork

sharp knife
table knife for spreading

INGREDIENTS

[1] 1 three-ounce package
    cream cheese, softened,
    or ⅓ cup cottage cheese
4 tablespoons cucumber,
    peeled and chopped
    (wrap and save the rest

    for a salad)
⅛ teaspoon salt
½ teaspoon chopped dill
    weed (fresh if you can
    get it)

[2] 1 three-ounce package
    cream cheese, softened,
    or ⅓ cup cottage cheese
¼ cup chopped dates or

    apricots or raisins
1 tablespoon chopped nuts
    or seeds

[3] 1 three-ounce package   chopped scallions
    cream cheese, softened,   (green onions)
      or ⅓ cup cottage cheese   2 tablespoons chopped
   1 tablespoon finely   celery

Make these three types of sandwiches with thin slices of Banana-Nut Loaf (page 17) or with any whole-grain bread. Use either cream cheese or cottage cheese. Cream cheese holds together better, especially for lunchbox sandwiches, but you should let it soften until it is at room temperature before you try to mix it. Each recipe makes enough filling for 2 or 3 sandwiches.

Put the cheese in a mixing bowl and mash it thoroughly with a fork. Add the rest of the ingredients and mix well. Spread on slices of bread. Add a lettuce leaf to each sandwich if you wish, and top with a second slice of bread.

THE FLOPSY BUNNIES'
VEGETABLE SANDWICHES

EQUIPMENT

small mixing bowl
fork
measuring cups and spoons

sharp knife
table knife for cutting

INGREDIENTS

[1] 1 small ripe avocado
   1 scallion (green onion)
   ½ teaspoon lemon juice
   ¼ teaspoon salt

1 or 2 tablespoons
   mayonnaise or sour
   cream
1 hard-cooked egg
   (see page 105)

Make these five sandwiches with any whole-grained bread. Each recipe makes enough filling for 2 or 3 sandwiches.

Cut the avocado in half, pull off the skin, and remove the seed. Put it in a mixing bowl and mash it with a fork. Chop the scallion finely and add it to the avocado. Add the lemon juice, salt, and mayonnaise or sour cream and mix well.

Chop the hard-cooked egg in rather large chunks and add it to the avocado mixture. Stir it in lightly.

Here are some other vegetable fillings:

INGREDIENTS

[2] 1 small ripe avocado	¼ cup wheat germ
½ ripe banana	2 tablespoons chopped
1 tablespoon lemon juice	nuts

Cut the avocado in half, pull off the skin, remove the seed, and put in a mixing bowl. Peel the banana, add it to the mixing bowl and mash both with a fork. Stir in the lemon juice, wheat germ, and nuts.

36

[3] 2 hard-cooked eggs
(see page 105)
¼ cup alfalfa sprouts
3 tablespoons chopped
pitted olives, if you
like them

¼ teaspoon dried sweet
basil, if you like it
¼ teaspoon salt
2 tablespoons mayonnaise
or sour cream

Put the eggs in a mixing bowl and mash them with a fork. Stir in the rest of the ingredients.

[4] ½ cup red or green
cabbage, cut up fine
2 tablespoons chopped
dried apricots or raisins

1 tablespoon chopped nuts
1-2 tablespoons mayon-
naise or sour cream

Put all the ingredients in a mixing bowl and stir.

[5] ⅔ cup canned, drained garbanzo beans (chick peas)
1 scallion (green onion)
2 tablespoons chopped celery
¼ teaspoon salt
1-2 tablespoons mayonnaise or sour cream

Put the garbanzos in a mixing bowl and mash them with a fork. Chop the scallion finely and add it to the garbanzos. Add the chopped celery, salt, and mayonnaise or sour cream.

NOTE: Also good for sandwich fillings: Carrot-Raisin salad (see page 58).

VEGETABLES

DUCHESS AND RIBBY'S
TOMATO-CHEESE PIE

EQUIPMENT

1 ½-quart casserole or baking
   dish
sharp knife
grater

wax paper or plate
measuring cups and spoons
mixing bowl
rotary beater

INGREDIENTS

butter or margarine
4 slices stale bread
2 medium tomatoes
¼ teaspoon sweet basil leaves
1 ½ cups cheese, grated
   cheddar, Swiss, or
   Mozzarella

2 eggs
1 cup milk
¾ teaspoon salt
¼ teaspoon pepper

Turn on the oven and let it heat to 350 degrees. Grease the casserole generously with butter or margarine.

Cut or tear the bread into small cubes and put them in the casserole.

Slice the tomatoes and arrange the slices over the cubed bread. Sprinkle the tomatoes with basil.

Grate the cheese onto a piece of wax paper or a plate, using the large openings on the grater. Pile the grated cheese loosely in the measuring cup to measure it. Spread it evenly over the tomato slices.

In a small mixing bowl beat the eggs with the milk. Add the salt and pepper. Pour the egg mixture over the cheese.

Bake for 35 to 40 minutes or until brown and bubbly.

Serves 4.

LITTLE BLACK RABBIT'S
ORANGE-HONEY CARROTS

EQUIPMENT

vegetable peeler   saucepan with lid
sharp knife   measuring cup and spoons

INGREDIENTS

6 carrots   ⅓ cup orange juice
1 tablespoon honey   ¼ teaspoon salt
3 tablespoons butter or   3 whole cloves
  margarine   1 tablespoon fresh parsley

Wash the carrots, scrape them with a vegetable peeler, and cut them into ½-inch slices with a sharp knife. Put them into a saucepan.

Add the honey, butter or margarine, orange juice, salt, and cloves. Put the lid on the saucepan and cook the carrots gently for 20 minutes, or until the carrots are tender when you test them with the tip of a knife.

Remove the lid, take out the cloves, and cook slowly until most of the juice has evaporated. Stir gently until the carrots are glazed with the butter and honey. Wash the parsley and cut it up fine. Sprinkle it over the carrots.

Serves 3 to 4.

PIGGERY PORCOMBE
GREEN BEANS AND MUSHROOMS

EQUIPMENT

saucepan with lid

sharp knife

medium-sized frying pan

fork

INGREDIENTS

2 cups fresh green beans cut in
    1-inch pieces, or 1 ten-ounce
    package of frozen green
    beans

1 small onion

½ tomato

½ cup chopped mushrooms

2 tablespoons oil

¼ teaspoon salt

2 tablespoons parsley, chopped

Cook fresh green beans following the directions on page 101, for 10 minutes. Or cook frozen green beans, following the directions on the package, for 3 minutes.

While the beans are cooking, chop the onion, tomato, and mushrooms.

Put the oil in the frying pan. Stir-fry the chopped vegetables, and the drained, partly cooked beans following the directions on page 104. Add salt, stir, and sprinkle with parsley.

Serves 3 or 4.

MR. McGREGOR'S
SCRUMPTIOUS PUREED BEETS

EQUIPMENT

small sharp knife
saucepan with lid

measuring cup and spoons
blender

INGREDIENTS

3 medium-sized beets
1 tablespoon chopped onion
2 tablespoons lemon juice

½ teaspoon salt
1 teaspoon honey
⅓ cup plain yogurt

Cut the roots and tops from the beets and wash the beets thoroughly. Following the directions on page 101, cook them in boiling water until tender—from 1 to 2 hours. Drain and cool. Slide off the skins, chop the beets into small pieces, and put them into the blender. Add the remaining ingredients to the blender, put on the lid, and run the blender until all the ingredients are well mixed. Serve hot or cold.

Serves 4.

OLD MR. BOUNCER'S
LEMON-MINT PEAS

EQUIPMENT

saucepan with lid
small skillet
small sharp knife

measuring spoons
mixing spoon

INGREDIENTS

1½ pounds fresh or
   1 ten-ounce package
   frozen peas
3 tablespoons butter

1 teaspoon lemon juice
1 teaspoon honey
2 tablespoons fresh mint,
   chopped

Shell the fresh peas and cook them following the directions on page 101. Or cook frozen peas following the directions on the package.

While the peas are cooking, melt the butter in a small skillet and add the lemon juice, honey, and mint. Cook slowly for 5 minutes. Add the peas to the mint mixture and stir.

Serves 3 to 4.

SALADS

ALDERMAN PTOLEMY TORTOISE'S SPINACH SALAD

E Q U I P M E N T

colander
paper towels
salad bowl and salad servers
sharp knife

measuring cup and spoons
fork
small mixing bowl

I N G R E D I E N T S

3 cups spinach
1 rib celery
1 hard-cooked egg (page 105)
1 scallion (green onion)

2 tablespoons sour cream
¼ teaspoon garlic salt
½ teaspoon lemon juice

Wash all the sand off the spinach under cool running water, drain in a colander, and pat dry with paper towels. Pull off the stems and tear the spinach into small pieces until you have about 3 cups. Put the spinach in a salad bowl.

Wash the celery and chop it in small pieces. Add it to the spinach.

In a small mixing bowl, mash the yolk of the hard-cooked egg with a fork. Chop the white in tiny pieces, chop the scallion, and add the white and scallion to the yolk. Add the sour cream, garlic salt, and lemon juice and stir until everything is well mixed.

Serve the dressing separately, or add it to the spinach and toss gently just until the leaves are coated with the dressing.

Serves 4.

53

PETER AND BENJAMIN'S
SUPER TOSSED SALAD

EQUIPMENT

colander

paper towels

plastic bag

sharp knife

measuring cups and spoons

small mixing bowl

teacup

salad bowl and salad servers

INGREDIENTS

2 cups fresh greens:
   iceberg, romaine, or
      Boston lettuce
   escarole

chicory

watercress

spinach

1 cup raw vegetables:
   red or green cabbage cut
      in small strips
   chopped celery

chopped scallions (green
      onions)

tomato cut in wedges

sliced carrots

sliced cauliflower
sliced mushrooms
peas, shelled
sliced avocado

sliced cucumbers
chopped green peppers,
   with the seeds removed
sprouts, fresh alfalfa or bean

1 cup leftover cooked
* vegetables:*
sliced carrots
potatoes cut in small cubes
peas
green beans

chopped beets
canned dried beans, drained,
   such as garbanzos, pinto
   beans, or kidney (red)
   beans

¼ *cup salad dressing:*
   3 tablespoons vegetable oil
   1 tablespoon vinegar or
      lemon juice
   ½ teaspoon salt

pepper
garlic powder
dried basil, thyme, or
   marjoram

garnishes:
   olives
   sliced hard-cooked egg
      (page 105)
   ½ cup croutons

1 tablespoon chopped
   parsley
1 tablespoon Parmesan
   cheese

Choose one kind of greens or a combination of two or three. Wash the greens under cool running water, drain in a colander, and pat dry with paper towels. Tear the greens in small pieces, wrap them loosely in damp paper towels, put them in a plastic bag, and store

56

in the refrigerator for half an hour, or until you are ready to use them. This makes them crisp.

Choose a combination of four or five vegetables, 1 cup raw and 1 cup cooked. Put them in a mixing bowl.

In a teacup mix the oil, vinegar, salt, pepper, and ½ teaspoon of whichever additional seasonings you like. Mix well and pour over the vegetables in the mixing bowl. Put in the refrigerator to chill.

When you are ready to serve the salad, put the greens in salad bowl and add the vegetables that have been soaking (marinating) in the salad dressing. Toss well. Decorate the salad with some of the garnishes.

Serves 4.

FIERCE BAD RABBIT'S
CARROT-RAISIN SALAD

vegetable peeler

grater and wax paper

sharp knife

large mixing bowl

measuring cups

mixing spoon

INGREDIENTS

2 carrots

2 apples

1 rib of celery

½ cup raisins

¼ teaspoon salt

1 teaspoon lemon juice

½ cup mayonnaise, sour
   cream or yogurt

¼ cup chopped nuts, if you
   like them

lettuce leaves

Wash the carrots and scrape with a vegetable peeler. Place a metal grater on a piece of wax paper and grate the carrots, using the large ice-cream-cone-shaped openings of the grater. Put the grated carrots in the mixing bowl.

Wash the apples, but do not peel them. Cut them in half and then in quarters. Cut out the core, and cut the apples into small pieces.

Wash the celery and chop it. Add the celery, apples, and raisins to the carrots. Sprinkle with salt and lemon juice. Stir in mayonnaise, sour cream, or yogurt.

Serve the salad on lettuce leaves and sprinkle with nuts if you like them.

Serves 4.

MRS. TIGGY-WINKLE'S TOMATOES STUFFED WITH COTTAGE CHEESE

EQUIPMENT

sharp knife

spoon

small mixing bowl

fork

INGREDIENTS

3 firm, ripe tomatoes

1 hard-cooked egg (page 105)

1 cup cottage cheese

⅓ cup sesame or sunflower
  seeds

2 tablespoons finely chopped
  scallions (green onions)

¼ teaspoon salt

lettuce leaves

Wash the tomatoes. Cut off the stem and carefully scoop out the seeds and pulp. (Save to use in soup or other recipe.)

Peel the egg and chop it into a small bowl. Add the cottage cheese, seeds, scallions, and salt. Mix well and spoon into the tomatoes. Serve the tomatoes on lettuce leaves. If some of the cheese mixture is left over, use it to make a spread for sandwiches or crackers.

Serves 3.

GINGER AND PICKLES'
BEAN SALAD

colander or strainer
can opener
sharp knife

mixing bowl
mixing spoon
measuring cups and spoons

1 medium-sized (14-to-21-
  ounce) can cooked dried
  beans, such as garbanzo
  beans (chick peas), navy
  beans, or kidney beans
1 rib celery *or* ½ green
  pepper, with the seeds
  removed

2 scallions (green onions)
1 small cucumber
2 tablespoons chopped parsley
¼ cup vegetable oil
1½ tablespoons vinegar
salt and pepper
Boston or romaine lettuce

Empty the canned beans into a colander or strainer and drain off
the liquid. Rinse the beans under cold running water. Let them
drain for a few minutes.

Meanwhile, wash the celery or pepper and chop it in small

pieces. Wash and chop the scallions. Peel the cucumber and chop it. Put the chopped vegetables in the mixing bowl and add the beans and parsley. Add the oil, vinegar, salt, and pepper and mix thoroughly.

Chill in the refrigerator for one hour to blend the flavors. Serve the salad on lettuce leaves.

Serves 4 to 6.

MR. JEREMY FISHER'S
CUCUMBER SALAD

EQUIPMENT

medium-sized mixing bowl   sharp knife
measuring cup and spoons

INGREDIENTS

2 cucumbers   ½ cup or more plain yogurt
4 tablespoons fresh mint *or*   ½ teaspoon salt
   2 scallions (green onions)   pepper

Peel the cucumbers and slice them thinly or cut them into small cubes.

   Chop the fresh mint or scallions and mix with the cucumber in a mixing bowl. Add yogurt and the salt and pepper.

   Cover and chill in the refrigerator for two hours, so that the flavor can develop and some of the excess water in the cucumbers can drain off. Pour off the accumulated water. Add more yogurt, if you wish.

Serves 4 to 6.

SOUPS

OLD MRS. RABBIT'S
HEARTY VEGETABLE SOUP

soup kettle

sharp knife

measuring cups and spoons

[1] *fresh vegetables:*
    cabbage, red or green
    carrots, scraped
    celery.
    corn, cut from the cob
    green beans
    lima beans, shelled
    onions, peeled

parsnips, peeled
peas, shelled
potatoes, peeled
tomatoes, with skin
    removed
turnips, peeled
zucchini

[2] *seasonings:*
    dried basil, thyme, and
        marjoram

fresh parsley
salt
pepper

[3] *canned beans:*
    kidney beans

white marrow beans

[4] *leafy greens:*
    escarole

spinach

For each cup of vegetables that you plan to use, put 2 cups of liquid in a soup kettle. The liquid can be plain water, water with added bouillon cubes (beef or vegetable), liquid saved from cooking vegetables or drained from canned vegetables, tomato juice, leftover strained beef broth, or canned beef broth, or a combination of any of these.

Use any combination of vegetables that you like. Wash the vegetables thoroughly. Cut the vegetables into small ($\frac{1}{4}$-inch to $\frac{1}{2}$-inch) cubes or slices. Add the raw vegetables to the liquid and bring to a boil.

Add the seasonings. For each cup of vegetables, add ½ teaspoon of any of the dried herbs, 1 tablespoon of chopped parsley, 1 teaspoon of salt, ¼ teaspoon of pepper. Cook slowly for ½ hour.

Add canned beans (drained) or any canned or leftover cooked vegetables. Cook for 10 more minutes.

Add fresh greens, such as spinach or escarole, which have been washed and torn into pieces, and cook for 5 minutes more.

Each cup of vegetables with 2 cups of water serves 2.

ANNA MARIA'S
CORN CHOWDER

EQUIPMENT

large saucepan with lid
measuring cup and spoon

sharp knife

INGREDIENTS

1 small onion
2 small ribs celery with leaves
4 cups chicken broth
(homemade, canned, or
made with 4 cups of water
and 4 chicken bouillon
cubes)

¾ teaspoon salt
⅛ teaspoon pepper
1½ cups corn (fresh and cut
off the cob, frozen, or
canned)
1 hard-cooked egg (page 105)
fresh parsley

With a sharp knife take the outer skin off the onion. Slice the onion into rings and then cut each of the slices into quarters. Cut the celery in ½-inch slices and chop up the leaves. Put them all in the saucepan with the chicken broth and salt and pepper. Cover the saucepan and simmer for ½ hour.

Add the corn (drained if canned) and simmer for 10 minutes.

Peel the egg and chop the egg in large chunks. Cut the parsley up fine. Add the egg and parsley to the soup and simmer for a few minutes until the egg is heated through.

Serves 4 to 6.

OLD MRS. PIG'S
POTATO SOUP

EQUIPMENT

sharp knife
large saucepan with lid

measuring cup and spoon
food mill or blender

INGREDIENTS

2 tablespoons butter or
  margarine
1 onion
3 medium-sized potatoes
2 cups water *or* chicken broth
  (homemade, canned, or

made with 2 cups of water
and 2 chicken bouillon
cubes)
1 teaspoon salt
1 rib celery, with leaves
2 cups milk

With a sharp knife take the outer skin off the onion. Slice the onion into rings and then cut each of the slices into quarters. Melt the butter or margarine in the saucepan and cook the onion slowly until it looks glassy. Do not let it brown.

Scrub the potatoes and peel them. Cut the potatoes in ½-inch slices and then cut each slice into cubes.

Put the potatoes in the saucepan and add the water or chicken broth, salt, and whole celery rib. Cover and cook slowly for 30 minutes, until the potatoes are very soft when you test them with the point of a sharp knife.

Remove the celery and discard it. Leave the potatoes in pieces, or put the mixture in a blender at medium speed for 10 seconds, or press it through a food mill.

Add the milk and heat the soup thoroughly, but do not let it boil or the milk will curdle and separate.

Serves 4 to 6.

CAT AND RAT
TOMATO SOUP

EQUIPMENT

medium-sized saucepan
measuring cup and spoons
sharp knife
mixing spoon

strainer
mixing bowl
4 soup mugs

INGREDIENTS

4 cups tomato juice
1 small onion, diced
½ rib of celery with leaves,
    diced
1 sprig of parsley
1 small bay leaf
1 teaspoon sugar

2 whole cloves
¼ teaspoon salt
dash of pepper
⅛ teaspoon sweet basil or
    marjoram
4 tablespoons of sour cream

76

Put all of the ingredients except the sour cream in the saucepan. Bring the mixture to a boil, turn the heat to low, and cook very slowly for fifteen minutes, stirring occasionally.

Pour the soup through the strainer into a mixing bowl. Divide the soup into four mugs and float one tablespoon of sour cream in each mug. Delicious hot or cold.

Serves 4.

NOTE: For a heartier soup, add 1 cup of leftover cooked vegetables, rice, or macaroni and serve in soup bowls.

DESSERTS

TOM KITTEN'S
HOMEMADE APPLESAUCE

EQUIPMENT

heavy saucepan with lid
small sharp knife
food mill

mixing spoon
measuring cups

INGREDIENTS

6 medium-sized tart apples
½ cup water

sugar or honey

Wash the apples. Cut them in half and then in quarters. You do not need to peel them or cut out the core because these will be left behind in the food mill.

Put the apples in the saucepan with the water. Put the lid on the pan. Cook them slowly, stirring occasionally, for 15 or 20 minutes, or until they feel tender when you test them with the point of a knife. Let them cool for 15 minutes more.

Set the food mill over a mixing bowl and press the apples and the cooking juice through.

The amount of sugar you need depends on the kind of apples you use and your own taste. Begin with ¼ cup of sugar or 2 tablespoons of honey, stirring it into the warm applesauce. Add more if you wish. Serve warm or cold or use in other recipes.

Cinnamon, cloves, nutmeg, raisins, and nuts are all good additions to plain applesauce.

Makes about 3 cups.

CECILY PARSLEY'S
SMOOTH APPLE CREAM

EQUIPMENT

measuring cups and spoons
2 small mixing bowls

rotary beater, or electric mixer
mixing spoon

INGREDIENTS

1 cup heavy cream
1 cup homemade applesauce
  (see page 80)
1 tablespoon honey

2½ tablespoons lemon juice
  (half of one lemon)
¼ teaspoon cinnamon
pinch of nutmeg

Chill the whipping cream, one mixing bowl, and the beater(s) thoroughly in the refrigerator. (This helps to keep the cream from turning to butter when you whip it, especially in warm weather.)

    In another mixing bowl put the applesauce, honey, lemon juice, cinnamon, and nutmeg and blend well.

Put the cream in the chilled bowl and beat it until it is very thick and stands up in stiff peaks when you lift the beater(s).

Fold the whipped cream into the applesauce by gently lifting and turning the mixture so you won't lose the air you have whipped into the cream.

Serve immediately or chill in the refrigerator. For a firmer texture, put it in the freezer for an hour, but do not let it stay longer or it will freeze.

Serves 4.

TABITHA TWITCHIT'S
SPICY RAISIN DESSERT

saucepan with lid
measuring cups and spoons
mixing spoon

sharp knife
cup

1½ cups raisins
¾ cup water
1 large apple
1 tablespoon cornstarch
½ teaspoon cinnamon

¼ teaspoon cloves
⅓ cup brown sugar
½ cup chopped walnuts or
   pecans, if you like them

Put the raisins in the saucepan with the water. Put the lid on the pan. Cook slowly for 5 minutes.

Wash the apple, but you do not need to peel it. Cut it in half and then in quarters. Cut out the core. Then cut it in small pieces and add these to the raisins. Cook for 5 minutes more.

Put the cornstarch in a cup and add a little cold water. Mix thoroughly and add to the raisins. Stir, cooking slowly, until the mixture thickens. Add the cinnamon, cloves, and brown sugar. Cook until the sugar melts.

Serve warm with plain or whipped cream. Sprinkle with walnuts or pecans if you like them.

Serves 4 to 6.

FLOPSY, MOPSY, AND COTTONTAIL'S FRESH BLUEBERRY COBBLER

EQUIPMENT

colander or strainer
medium-sized saucepan
measuring cups and spoons
baking dish (9 x 9)
medium-sized mixing bowl

fork
two dinner knives or a pastry
   blender
pot holders
hot mat or wire rack

INGREDIENTS

1 pint blueberries
¼ cup water
¾ cup granulated white or
   raw sugar
1 cup whole-wheat flour

¾ cup brown sugar, loosely
   packed
½ teaspoon salt
1 teaspoon baking powder
pinch of nutmeg
⅓ cup butter or margarine

Turn on the oven and let it heat to 350 degrees.

Wash the blueberries in a colander or strainer and pick out any stems and leaves. Put the blueberries, water, and white or raw sugar in a saucepan and bring to a boil stirring so sugar does not burn. Simmer for two minutes. Pour the slightly cooked berries into the baking dish.

In the mixing bowl put the flour, brown sugar, salt, baking powder, and nutmeg and mix them thoroughly with a fork.

Add the butter or margarine, cut into small pieces. Use a pastry blender, or use two knives, one in each hand, and cut the butter

or margarine into the flour mixture until it forms crumbs about the size of peas.

Sprinkle the crumbs over the berries. Bake for 25 minutes, or until the crumbs are light brown. Use the pot holders to remove the baking dish from the oven. Set the dish on a hot mat or wire rack to cool slightly.

Serve with plain or whipped cream or vanilla ice cream.

Serves 4 to 6.

NOTE: You can use other fresh fruit instead of blueberries—such as pitted cherries, raspberries, sliced ripe peaches, sliced apples, or rhubarb cut into ½-inch pieces.

LITTLETOWN-FARM
CARROT COOKIES

vegetable peeler
sharp knife
measuring cups and spoons
saucepan with lid
2 medium-sized mixing bowls
fork

cookie sheets
mixing spoon
pot holders
spatula
wire racks

5 carrots
¾ cup water (more if carrots
   go dry)
salt
1 cup unbleached white flour
1 cup whole-wheat flour
2½ teaspoons baking powder
¼ teaspoon cinnamon
⅛ teaspoon nutmeg

½ teaspoon salt
½ cup soft vegetable
   shortening
½ cup butter or margarine
1 cup brown sugar
2 eggs
¾ cup golden raisins
extra shortening

Wash the carrots, scrape them with a vegetable peeler, rinse and cut them into ¼-inch round slices with a sharp knife. Measure 1½ cups of carrot slices and put them into a small saucepan. Add the water and a pinch of salt, cover, and cook for 15 to 20 minutes over medium heat or until the carrots are tender when you test them with the tip of a knife. Drain the cooking water and save to use in soup.

Turn on the oven and let it heat to 400 degrees.

While the carrots are cooking put the white flour, whole-wheat flour, baking powder, cinnamon, nutmeg, and salt in a mixing bowl. Stir them lightly with a fork until they are thoroughly mixed. Put the cooked carrots in another mixing bowl and mash them with a fork. Add the soft shortening, butter or margarine,

and brown sugar and mix well. Beat in the 2 eggs.

Add the dry ingredients to the carrot mixture and stir until they are completely blended. Stir in the raisins.

Grease 2 cookie sheets with the extra soft shortening. Use a spoon to drop the cookie mixture on the sheets about 2 inches apart. Bake 10 minutes. Use pot holders to take the cookie sheets from the oven. Remove the cookies from the cookie sheets with a spatula and put them on wire racks to cool.

Makes 4 dozen 3-inch cookies.

THE DORMOUSE CHILDREN'S
NUTTY FROZEN BANANA

EQUIPMENT

wax paper

INGREDIENTS

1 ripe banana   2 tablespoons finely chopped nuts

Spread the nuts on a piece of wax paper. Peel the banana. Lay the banana on the wax paper. Cup the banana in one hand and carefully press the chopped nuts into it so that they stick. Place the nut-covered banana, still on the wax paper, in the freezer for at least one hour. Serve whole and frozen.

Serves 1.

SIMPKIN'S GLOUCESTER TOWN GRANOLA COOKIES

EQUIPMENT

1 small mixing bowl
1 medium-sized
   mixing bowl
measuring cups and spoons
fork
mixing spoon

teaspoon
cookie sheets
pot holders
spatula
wire racks

INGREDIENTS

½ cup room temperature
   butter or margarine
½ cup brown sugar
½ cup granulated white
   or raw sugar
1 egg
1 tablespoon milk

1 teaspoon vanilla
1 cup whole-wheat flour
½ teaspoon baking powder
½ teaspoon baking soda
½ teaspoon salt
1 cup granola (page 22)
   or oatmeal

Turn on the oven and let it heat to 350 degrees.

Put the butter or margarine, brown sugar, and white or raw sugar in the medium-sized mixing bowl and mix well with a fork. Add the egg and beat it in. Stir in the milk and the vanilla.

In the small mixing bowl, put the flour, baking powder, baking soda, and salt. Stir them lightly with a fork until they are thoroughly mixed.

Add the dry ingredients to the butter mixture and stir until they are completely blended. Add the granola or oatmeal and mix it well.

Drop the dough from a teaspoon onto ungreased cookie sheets. Bake 10 minutes until they are light brown. Use pot holders to take the cookie sheets from the oven. Remove the cookies from the cookie sheets with a spatula and put them on wire racks to cool.

Makes 3 dozen cookies.

PETER AND BEATRIX'S SPECIAL CHRISTMAS FUDGY PUDDING CAKE

2 medium-sized mixing bowls
measuring cups and spoons
fork
small saucepan

8-inch-square baking pan
mixing spoon
pot holders
hot mat or wire rack

1 cup unbleached white flour
¾ cup wheat germ
¾ cup granulated white or
   raw sugar
2 teaspoons baking powder
¼ teaspoon salt
2 tablespoons butter or
   margarine

⅔ cup milk
1 teaspoon vanilla
1 cup brown sugar, firmly
   packed
½ cup unsweetened cocoa or
   carob powder
2 cups hot tap water

Turn on the oven and let it heat to 350 degrees.

In one mixing bowl put the flour, wheat germ, white or raw sugar, baking powder, and salt. Stir them lightly with a fork until they are thoroughly mixed.

Melt the butter or margarine in a small saucepan and add it to the dry ingredients along with the milk and vanilla. Pour the batter in the ungreased baking pan.

In another mixing bowl put the brown sugar and cocoa or carob powder. Stir with a fork until they are thoroughly mixed. Sprinkle the brown sugar mixture evenly over the batter.

Carefully pour the hot tap water over the brown sugar mixture. *Do not stir!* Set the pan in the oven and bake for 45 minutes. Use

the pot holders to remove the baking pan from the oven. Set the pan on a hot mat or wire rack to cool slightly.

While the pudding bakes, the fudgy sauce settles to the bottom of the pan and the cake-like mixture rises to the top. Make sure to dip some of the sauce over each serving. Serve warm with whipped cream.

Serves 6.

SOME MORE
HELPFUL
HINTS

HOW TO COOK VEGETABLES

Fresh vegetables keep their fresh flavor, bright color, and healthful vitamins when they are cooked quickly, either by boiling in a little water or by stir-frying in a small amount of hot oil.

First wash the vegetables. Pick out and discard any that are not in good condition. Cut off stem ends. Some vegetables should be cooked with their skins on to keep the vitamins; others may be peeled or scraped. Boil the vegetables whole, or cut them in small pieces for boiling or stir-frying. Small pieces cook faster.

HOW TO BOIL VEGETABLES

sharp knife
vegetable peeler

medium-sized saucepan
with lid

Put an inch of water in the saucepan and add ½ teaspoon of salt. Bring the water to a boil. Add the prepared vegetables and bring to a boil again. Cook slowly over low heat until the vegetables are just tender but still crisp when you test them with the sharp point of a knife.

Be careful not to overcook vegetables. Some people like them crunchier than others, but nobody likes them when they are limp and mushy. Save the water in which they were cooked to use in soups or stews.

You can dress up vegetables with herbs, such as parsley or basil, or with garnishes such as nuts or hard-cooked eggs, or with sauces made with cream or lemon. But this is a guide for serving them plain, with only butter or margarine and perhaps a little freshly ground pepper.

101

Some vegetables are also good served cold in a salad with mayonnaise or oil and vinegar dressing.

Asparagus: Break in 1-inch pieces. Cook lower stalks for 10 minutes; add tips and cook 5 more minutes.

Beets: Cook whole and unpeeled for 30 to 45 minutes and let cool in cooking water a few minutes to keep color. Run cold water over the cooked beets and slip off the skins.

Carrots: Scrub, cut in slices. Cook 10 to 20 minutes.

Corn: Cook cobs 5 minutes in *unsalted* water (salt toughens corn).

Green Beans: Leave whole or cut in 1-inch pieces. Cook for 15 to 20 minutes.

Peas: Shell peas. Cook 8 to 10 minutes with a few pods for flavor.

Potatoes: Peel and cut up large potatoes but leave small new potatoes whole with skins on. Cook 20 to 25 minutes.

Sweet Potatoes: Cut up, leaving skins on. Cook 20 to 25 minutes. Remove skins after cooking.

Tomatoes: Dip for a few moments in small pan of boiling water and remove with slotted spoon. Cut in quarters and cook without water for 8 to 10 minutes.

Zucchini: Cut in slices and leave unpeeled. Cook about 5 minutes.

HOW TO STIR-FRY VEGETABLES

EQUIPMENT

sharp knife

medium-sized frying pan
   with lid

vegetable peeler

wooden mixing spoon or
   spatula

Put 2 tablespoons of vegetable oil in the pan. Heat the oil over high heat. Add vegetables and stir them quickly without stopping for 2 or 3 minutes, or until just crisp and tender.

Some vegetables need longer cooking than others. Boil hard vegetables, such as carrots and cauliflower, for 10 minutes and drain carefully before stir-frying.

HOW TO HARD COOK AN EGG

saucepan with lid   timer
pot holder

Put several eggs in a saucepan, so there is space between the eggs. Cover them with cold water. Cook them over medium heat until the water boils. Then put the lid on the saucepan and turn off the heat. Set the timer for 25 minutes.

Run cold water over the eggs. This makes them easier to handle and easier to remove the shells.

HOW TO LIKE ONIONS

Many young people claim they don't like onions, even though they may enjoy the flavor when the onions are cooked or mixed with other ingredients. If you think you don't like onions, remember that the trick is to use the right kind of onion for the recipe and to prepare it correctly.

Scallions, also called green onions or spring onions, are among the mildest flavored onions, and are often used raw in salads. Slice them crosswise—you can use both the white and green parts.

The leek, which looks like the scallion but is much much larger, is often used in soups. It has a mild flavor.

Red onions have a strong flavor and add color to salads.

Bermuda onions, which are large and white, are sliced thinly for sandwiches, especially hamburgers.

Yellow onions, the most common and usually sold by the bagful, are often used in soups and stews rather than raw in salads. You will enjoy their flavor more if you chop them very finely and cook them thoroughly.

The chive is a member of the onion family. The green spikes are sometimes chopped finely and used raw like parsley.

106

HOW TO CHOP

EQUIPMENT

sharp knife (a paring knife with
   a blade about 6 inches long)

wooden cutting board

Many ingredients need to be cut into small pieces before they are
used in recipes—sometimes to make them cook faster, and some-

times to make them easier to eat or more attractive to look at.

Please remember to be very careful each time you use a knife and to have a grown-up assist you.

To chop leafy things such as parsley or mint, lay the leaves on the cutting board in a bunch and cut through the whole bunch, starting at one end and drawing the knife toward you. Use your free hand to keep the bunch in place as you cut.

To chop long narrow vegetables such as scallions or celery, lay one at a time on the cutting board with the leafy end to the left (if you are right-handed). Holding the vegetable in place, cut it into two or three long strips with the tip of the knife. Then cut across these strips. To make very small pieces, make the cross cuts very close together.

To chop rounded things such as eggs or mushrooms, first cut one in half and place the flat cut sides down on the board. Then cut the halves into slices. Turn the board and cut across the slices. Or you can slice both eggs and mushrooms in an egg slicer.

To chop nuts, arrange a few at a time in a single layer. Hold the tip of the knife in the fingers of your left hand and the handle in your right (if you are right-handed) and press the knife straight down through the nuts. Move the knife about $\frac{1}{4}$ inch and press it down again. Push the nuts and pieces close together as they begin to spread apart. Repeat several times until all the nuts are chopped.

SOURCES OF ILLUSTRATIONS

INDEX